SWIM

Sheila Fraser

Illustrations by Lisa Kopper

BARRON'S
New York · Toronto

My name's Jerry. I'm learning how to swim. Every week I come to the swimming pool with my Mom and my friend Sean.

We change into our swimsuits
in a big room. I put my clothes and shoes
in a locker and Mom keeps the key.
She tells us not to peek at other people
because it's rude.

Victoria waves and so does little Jodi.
Sean's swimmies are blown up a lot.
Mine are hardly blown up at all.
Mom says they've got enough air in them.
But I'm not sure. It's kind of scary
when they don't hold you up much.

It's cold when you first get in the water.
Mom says, "Once you get in you'll be O.K."

She takes turns helping me and Sean.
I kick with my legs and sometimes I splash her
in the face. She doesn't seem to mind. She says
I'm nearly ready to try without swimmies,
but I'm not so sure.

Carmel swims up and down
doing what she calls the "crawl."
She can swim a whole length of the pool.
She wears goggles like real swimmers do.

Nicholas can float and swim on his back.
I'll be able to do that one day too.
Right now my best stroke is the doggy paddle.

When Mom helps Sean, I try on my own.
I don't like getting my face wet
but Mom says to try blowing bubbles
on the water. That's fun.

Now I must remember to kick my feet
and paddle with my arms.
There's more to swimming
than just blowing bubbles.

Whaaa .... I've got water up my nose
and I've swallowed some too. It tastes yucky.

Sean says I'm a big baby. It's easy for him —
he's got air in his swimmies. I'll show him.

"I'm going to take off these swimmies
and swim on my own."
Mom says, "O.K., there's hardly any air
in them anyway."
She must think I can swim without them.

Why is everybody looking at me?
I could do it if they went away.
But I'm going to show that Sean.
I'll just try one stroke .... or maybe two ....

I can see Mom smiling.
She says, "Come on – that's it."

I kick with my legs and pull with my hands.
But it feels funny without swimmies
and I put my feet down.